For Alex, Nora & Wilf, Noah & Hattie,
Zoë & Felix, James & Mollie –
Karl Newson

For Baby Kaszás and her mummy –
Louise Pigott

This edition published by Parragon Books Ltd in 2018 and distributed by

Parragon Inc.
440 Park Avenue South, 13th Floor
New York, NY 10016
www.parragon.com

Copyright © Parragon Books Ltd 2018

Written by Karl Newson
Illustrated by Louise Pigott
Edited by Lily Holland
Designed by Kathryn Davies
Production by Jon Wakeham

ISBN 978-1-4748-9228-5

Printed in China

Little Gray's
BIRTHDAY SURPRISE

PaRragon

Bath · New York · Cologne · Melbourne · Delhi
Hong Kong · Shenzhen · Singapore

On the morning of Little Gray's birthday
he awoke with a "Hop hop hooray!"

He crunched his breakfast carrot,
and he hopped outside to play.

He beamed the biggest smile
with his fluffy ears raised high.

"Come back home for lunch!" said Mom.
"We're having carrot pie!"

He bounded through the butterflies
and flowers in the sun.

Then all the way to Fox's house
to have some birthday fun.

DO NOT
DISTURB

"Do not disturb" read Fox's door.
Perhaps he was asleep?

So Little Gray went on his way,
hop! skip! leap!

His fluffy ears weren't quite so high
as he bounced through rays of light.
Then all the way to Squirrel's house,
but …

… Squirrel was out of sight.
"Not at home" read Squirrel's door.
Could she be at the shop?

Not at
home
x

So Little Gray went on his way,
boing! bounce! hop!

His fluffy ears fell lower
as he jumped through fields of green.
Then all the way to Bear's house,
but …

... Bear was nowhere to be seen.

"Out all day" the notice read,
but where could Bear have gone?

Little Gray's ears drooped
down,
down,
down ...

Out
all day
x

… and he sighed.
"Where is everyone?"

He felt so sad all on his own,
so lonely and so small.
"My friends have forgotten my birthday.
This isn't fun at all!"

"hello!"

He called them in his
loudest voice ...

... but there was no reply.

He curled himself up in a ball.
A tear fell from his eye.

Then he felt a tingle,
from his nose down to his tail.

Great big

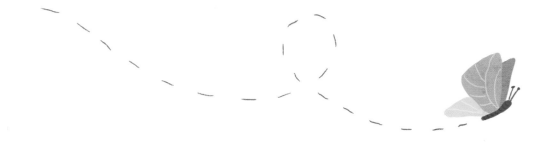

footprints **on** the ground ...
the

Bear had left a trail!

A trail that led through fields of green,

and back through rays of light,

back through flowers and butterflies,

to a happy, hoppy sight ...

Surprise!

Squirrel, Bear, and Fox had planned
a party all along!
All his friends were there with Mom
to sing his birthday song.

♪ **Happy Birthday to You!** ♪

A bouncy castle, cake, and hats,
the fun went on all day!

Little Gray beamed the
biggest smile and cheered,

"Hop hop hooray!"